Backpack Stories

Annie Levin

First Printing 2014

Copyright © 2014 Annie Levin

All rights reserved under International Copyright Law. Reproduction of text or cover in whole or in part without the express written consent by the author is not permitted and is unlawful according to the 1976 Untied States Copyright Act.

Printed in the United States of America

Backpack Stories
ISBN-13: 978-1505558432
ISBN-10: 1505558433

CONTENTS

Brushing Twice a Day Keeps Dentists Away

I've always dreaded going to the dentist. I hate the fact that someone is looking in my mouth. The dentist searches as if she's looking for gold; she picks at my gums and sometimes she scrapes my teeth so that it feels like she is trying to "create" a cavity!

The thing I fear the most would be getting a filling. I know that it's good for me, and that otherwise my tooth would rot, but it's just a very unpleasant feeling. I always try to take super precautions when brushing my teeth, so that I don't have to come back, but somehow my dentist manages to see me again and again.

So here I was, in the middle of a sunny April day, celebrating my Spring break with reading on my parents' king-sized bed. No worries in the air. No homework to be done. Then we got THE call. The automated voice announced Dr. Sarian.

"My dentist! Is she missing me again?"

My stomach tightened as my dad peaked into the room:

"Sweetie, got a minute? Dr. Sarian's secretary called. They have an opening and we can actually come in for your filling **tomorrow**!"

His face was gleaming. I was disgusted. That appointment wasn't due until June. I didn't want to go tomorrow - not during my Spring BREAK!

"So, what did you say?" I asked him with suspicion.

"Nothing. She is still on the phone, but muted. You wanna go?"

I wasn't sure what to say. I really didn't want to go,

but then…after this I wouldn't have to come back until our six-month checkup…Six months without Dr. Sarian sounded like a dream! I was in.

"Okay, Dad."

"Great!" And with that he left the room.

The next morning I woke up early. I was hungry and aware: When you are getting a filling there isn't much on the menu to eat. You get to enjoy Dr. Sarian's specialty: DRY toast and apple juice. It felt like a stone drowning on the bottom of my stomach. However, Dr. Sarian would approve.

~

As we stepped into the building of Dr. Sarian's office, I got a nervous sensation inside. I definitely was not excited. My dad and I walked into the quiet waiting room and took a seat. I observed all the other small kids playing with toys or watching Frozen on TV, unaware of what was to come. Before long I could see the nurse walking toward the door. She was of average height, thin, and had blonde hair fixed in a tight ponytail. She looked like a confident person. She peaked out and called me. Obediently I got up and my dad trailed behind.

"I'm sorry Dad, but we don't let the parents in the same room when we do fillings. You can stay here."

Her voice was cold but she said it with a smile. I was not happy with this arrangement and I didn't like her smile either. My dad reassured me that it would be all right and sat back down on his chair. This left me and "Blondie" as buddies…but she was not my buddy! She closed the door and we started walking down the long hall of rooms.

She was in a good mood - as all Dr. Sarian's nurses seemed to be. We passed many rooms filled with children in them. Some cried as if something torturous was being done to them; others were deadly quiet.

"So, do you brush your teeth after every meal?" the nurse tested me.

"Well, not after **every** meal but definitely twice a day," I replied honestly with a smile.

She frowned. This was obviously not the reply she was hoping for.

"Well you know that food settles between your teeth when you eat and if you don't brush them after every meal then it can cause cavities. That's why it's recommended to brush your teeth as often as possible."

Of course I knew that — I wasn't a careless five-year old! I did take good care of my teeth but I guess I wasn't as enthusiastic about them as she appeared to be.

Brushing Twice a Day Keeps Dentists Away

"Are you flossing too?"

I didn't want to answer.

"Oh, when will we be there?"

The hall wasn't very long, but it seemed like it went on for ages. Finally, before I could come up with a reply she turned into our room. I was relieved.

"Sit down here, please."

She patted the dentistry chair and grabbed a pillow and blanket from a nearby stool. As soon as I sat down, she got to work. First she lowered the chair to almost a laying position. Then, she placed the pillow behind my head. I approved.

"Next give me ice-cream and we'll be BFF's," I thought.

"Sit still," she said.

Then, she tucked me in the blanket.

"It's very soft," I complimented.

"Haha, yes I know."

She picked up a pink pig-nosed looking object that was connected to a tube. The tube traveled behind my chair and then connected to some tank of a sort - this was for the "happy gas". Then my "assistant" carefully put it on my nose. She went back to the tank and it sounded like she was pumping something.

This resulted in small puffs of air flowing through the tube up into my nose.

"Take deep breaths," she instructed.

I did as I was told. It smelled like bubble gum.

"Ok now, sit still and wait here, Hun.   I'm gonna get Dr. Sarian." She walked out of the room.

I kept breathing; with every breath I took, I felt more and more drowsy.   I closed my eyes and listened to the sounds of the other busy nurses and patients. My mind was peacefully drifting away.

I was still half asleep, when a sharp pinch let me

know Dr. Sarian was near. I couldn't say "Hi" for something weird was lodged into my mouth.

"Hold nice and still for me," she said with deep concentration.

I knew what this was - the Novocain - and although I was in a very uncomfortable position, I didn't dare move for the sake of accidentally getting shot somewhere else.

"Excellent job," the nurse reassured several times, "We are almost done!"

Unable to respond, I just took another deep breath and dove into the world of bubble-gum.

I positively decided that getting this filling wasn't so bad after all.

The Game

It was finally here. The day I was waiting for. The day my favorite game's sequel, Metro Brody 2, would finally come to the stores. I couldn't wait. I just had to get outside and line up at GameStop. I just HAD to get the game!

Ever since the company announced they were going to make a sequel to Metro Brody, I started to save. I saved EVERY penny I earned from chores or from mowing Mrs. Perk's yard. I even held a lemonade stand with my best friend Mark that included my sister's cheerleading group (my genius plan of course). Saving was fun, but now it was time to spend it all; it was time to spend everything I earned over the past summer. I quickly jumped out of bed, got changed and grabbed my wallet. I wasn't hungry. Too excited to talk to Gram and Pap, I made my way to the door. I was going to get Metro Brody 2!

After a while of standing in line, I was bored. The fresh morning air was still crisp from the previous cold night. Somebody coughed. I heard a baby cry. Looking up ahead of me, I tried to see where the snake of people started and how fast it moved. I saw Le Café, my Aunt Monica's china shop and a beauty salon. I could only see the shape of a building way up ahead. It was GameStop. That meant this would be a long wait.

Some people were talking, texting, staring, daydreaming and more. I kept looking around the crowd searching for something that would keep me entertained. Just then I spotted something interesting; VERY interesting actually. It was Mark!

He was up ahead of me (about fifty people). If I got his attention, maybe I could skip ahead and stand right next to him in line! I wanted to text him to ask and see what he'd say. I reached into my pocket for my phone… I forgot it!

"Aw Man!" I said out loud.

The Game

Everyone around me stared. I could feel my face turning red.

I hesitated for a moment and finally said, "...I stepped on gum. These WERE new sneakers too!"

That was the lamest thing ever but at least everybody stopped looking at me.

I still really wanted to talk to Mark. He was close to the end so if he agreed then this would be a way of getting the game sooner. There HAD to be some way to get his attention. I tried waving, but I got no response. He was just too busy kicking the dirt below his feet.

Finally he looked this way!

"MARK!" I called out waving, "Over here!"

He looked the other way. Something got his attention. A man was directing him to go inside a big glass door. No!

I must have said it out loud again because another set of a hundred eyes were staring. I tried to look as serious as possible. When they realized nothing interesting was going on with me, they all looked away.

I had been waiting for hours. All I wanted was a simple game. I had the money and everything. I just wished I had some kind of VIP pass. Then I could be the first person in line to get the game and then run home to play it.

Someone pushed me and my daydreaming came to an end.

"Move it kid." He grunted.

"Oops, sorry." I quickly got back into my place.

I was on the hill now. I looked behind and saw the line of people go on forever.

It was an hour or two later (I was losing count) and the sun was blazing on my head. I saw a lot of people opening their bags and lunchboxes having their snack. It made me hungry.

I wished I brought a snack or that I could just hop out of line and buy a sandwich from Le Café. That wasn't an option though because even if I bribed someone to hold my place in line, the café was far from sight. I left the plaza a while ago and it would be too long of a walk. Now I was by all of the big shops: the mall, PetSmart, DW Shoe Storage and **GameStop**. I was almost there!

Soon enough I will have my own copy of Metro Brody 2 in my hands and I will be able to play!

So many people had passed me with Metro Brody 2 in their hands.

What if no more copies are left by the time I get to the building? What if Mark gets it but not me? My brain raced. I didn't want to be left out of the fun at school!

I overheard some people near me murmuring about the game.

"How soon do you think a new shipment would take if they ran out?"

"I don't know," answered the other, "Probably a few weeks. It could take two or three to get an order this big again."

This worried me. Now I REALLY wanted some VIP pass.

About half an hour passed, again, and I was still in line. Luckily, there were only about ten people in front of me now. I was thrilled!

A worker came out of GameStop. He was trying to tell everyone something.

Uh oh! I hope he isn't saying what I think he is.

People started walking away. They were leaving the line!

"NO!" I cried.

I rushed to the door before the man went back inside.

"Sir, please don't tell me that you ran out of Metro Brody 2!"

"Sorry, kid, but we did," he replied. "Come back in about three weeks and we will have a new order shipped in. If you preordered a copy then come inside and I can give it to you straight away."

The news was unbearable. All that time waiting in line was WASTED! By the time the order comes in, school would start and I wouldn't have any time to play. I was crushed.

Alas, two weeks went by, but still no news of Metro Brody 2 being shipped in. School had started, and about almost all the boys in my class had the game. I had visited Mark a couple times and tried the game with him, but it felt weird. It wasn't MY game... It was his. One day after school, I walked over to my locker to collect my belongings. I couldn't help but notice that it seemed a bit open.

Did someone try to steal something of mine?

When I opened it, a small, thin wrapped package fell down by my feet.

Eh, Gina probably just returned my book.

But then a little written note caught my eye:

> To: My best friend Zach
> From: Mark Lane

The Game

I unwrapped the gift. I couldn't believe what I was seeing!

In my hands was my very own copy of something I've really been wanting; something that I kept on trying to get for a long time.

That something was...
the game!

A Visit Next Door

I was going nuts. Freedo was chewing the piano bench leg. I turned around to see James adding something into the boiling pot of noodles, and Laurel was nowhere in sight.

I was just about to scream when the phone rang –

Backpack Stories

Ok, let me start from the beginning:

My name is Katness Miller - but everyone calls me Kat. I am 14 years old. This is a story of what happened to me last April, when I was babysitting the Peterson kids: Laurel and James.

I had been saving all the money I had for a new phone. I already saved $200, but I needed a bunch more. My solution was a raise in allowance. I calculated how long it would take if my parents raised it to $30 per month and decided it was the way to go. For girls like me, there were no jobs waiting around. I had a case. Yes, I could imagine the tightened white lips of my dad shredding the word "No!" but I prepared myself for the next morning's speech anyway.

~

The next morning I was all excited. I got dressed, brushed my hair and presented myself downstairs, only to find that no one was in sight.

"Where is everybody?" I wondered.

It was 10:00 AM and by now, everyone would've been up. I noticed a note:

Dear Kat,

I took Abbey to the store with me to buy meat for lunch and Dad had to take his car for an oil change. We'll be back shortly. Please make yourself breakfast!

Xoxo

-Mom

Then the phone rang.

"Hello?" I asked.

"Oh, Kat, it's you! I dialed the right number after all," replied a familiar voice - It was Mrs. Peterson, our neighbor.

"Well, good morning, Mrs. Peterson!"

"Oh goodness gracious! Ever since I woke up today everything is going wrong. I was hoping you could help me."

"Sure, but how?"

"You see, I have a hair appointment that I was waiting for a whole month. Unfortunately, my husband's boss called him to the office so I have no one to watch the kids. Oh, dear, I was hoping you could watch the kids for just a few hours - from four to six. Dave should be home by then."

I wasn't sure what to say. Part of me felt bad for her, but the other part was still focused on the phone.

"I know this is of short notice, and you may not be able to, but if it's possible I would be willing to pay you $50." She added.

Well that sounded like a deal! Watching a couple kids for only two hours and getting that reward was great. It sure felt like the jackpot to me.

"I'd love to." I replied with a smile.

"Oh thank you so much!" she rejoiced. I could practically see her dancing on the other end.

~

A Visit Next Door

"Welcome Kat," Mrs. Peterson greeted, "Do, please, come inside."

She led me to the counter of a cherry colored cabinet and white tiled kitchen. It was lovely and neat. Her children were sitting by the table quietly, staring at me.

"Ok, everything you need to know is here on the kitchen isle," she explained, "Oh, and one more thing: No one can touch the piano."

That sounded a bit odd to me, but I understood. It would be such a shame if something happened to it.

She smiled, "Now I really must go. Make yourself at home, Katness, and kids, you MUST listen to her."

We bid goodbye, and she kissed her kids. She headed towards the garage door when James grabbed her leg and pulled the other way.

"I don't want you to go!" he pleaded, "I DON'T!!"

"James, honey, please!"

Mrs. Peterson tried peeling his fingers off one at a time. James wouldn't budge. With a little pull, I managed to pick him up and bring him back to the counter. He started kicking and screaming. Mrs. Peterson looked troubled, but I signaled her to go. As soon as I heard the garage close, I let the little "beast" down. He ran to the garage door but couldn't open it.

He stomped his feet and ran upstairs. I was left with Laurel.

"Ok Laurel, what do *you* want to do?"

She shrugged her shoulders but didn't say a word.

"Are you hungry?" I suggested in doubt.

She nodded.

I peered at Mrs. Peterson's list:

Freedo:

Take him out whenever needed (only in the back lawn)

PS: You don't need to feed him

Food for kids:

As a snack give the kids a sandwich, and for dinner just spaghetti.

Pasta noodles - in the pantry (Laurel can show you)

Spaghetti sauce - in the fridge

"Alright, what kind of sandwich would you like?"

Laurel got up and left the room.

"Oh, how rude!" I thought.

A Visit Next Door

She came back with a loaf of bread, peanut butter, and jelly. Apparently she had paid a visit to the pantry.

"Ok then, want to he-"

There was a big **thud** upstairs. Laurel and I ran upstairs into James' room. To our surprise it wasn't him - he had fallen asleep from all the crying.

"Then who made that-"

Again, we heard another **thud**; this time coming from the room next door - the bathroom.

I was scared out of my socks. Someone was trying to break in!

"Stand back." I told Laurel.

I grabbed a nearby umbrella and threw open the bathroom door…a little Jack Russell terrier jumped in my face.

"Freedo!" Laurel exclaimed and picked him up.

I headed downstairs to finish Laurel's sandwich.

~

About an hour had gone by. Laurel was now coloring, James was still sleeping and I was reading a book on the couch. Everything was well.

"Ahhhhh! Mr. Tudels is gooone!" James cried running to me, "Gone!"

His face was in tears.

"Who's Mr. Tuttles?" I asked him.

"No, Mr. Tudels!"

"Oh, Mr. Tudels. Who is that?"

I could see James was frustrated, and even more upset because he thought I was teasing him.

"Freedo has him!" he called and ran to catch the thief.

"Laurel, who is Mr. Tudels…or however you pronounce it?"

"He's James' old, beat-up teddy bear. It's really called Mr. Cuddles, but James can't pronounce it yet." She explained.

"Great. A wild goose chase around the house."

I went to find the dog.

~

James was running from room to room upstairs chasing after a brown and white rocket. I stopped at the bottom of the steps.

A Visit Next Door

"James, stop running. You could get hurt."

He ran out of his room chasing Freedo.

"But I-"

He ran into Laurel's room…he came out.

"…need-"

He ran into a bathroom….he came out.

"…Mr. T-"

He ran into his parents' room...he ran down the steps and I grabbed him.

"…TUDDELS."

He tried to escape my grasp, but I didn't let him.

"Listen, James, I'm sure your mom doesn't like it when you run. I know you **really** want Mr. Cuddles, so I'll help you, but promise me you won't run."

"Ok, okay. Hurry!"

I placed the boy down and we split in opposite directions. Trapping Freedo was the best plan.

"Come here Freedo," I called, "Here doggie, doggie."

I saw him. Chewing lavishly on one of Mr. Cuddles' ears, he growled. He watched my every move.

"Ah, a distraction should work." I thought

"James, distract Freedo."

James obeyed and started hammering at the door. As an instinct, Freedo got up to see what the matter was leaving poor Mr. Cuddles alone on the carpet. I dove into the air, head first, smudging my face into a disgustingly foul smelling "sponge." There it was: an old, beat up, "tailless squirrel", balancing between my two fingers.

"Thank you, Katy!" James leaped with joy and started smothering Mr. Cuddles in hugs and kisses.

I glanced at Freedo, who now looked as if he had lost something special. He turned around, kicked his back leg and left.

"My, what attitude that dog has!"

~

At last, everyone was behaving the right way. Laurel and I chatted, and we played a game with James as well. Finally, everything was going the way I hoped.

But then, spoiled little **Freedo** broke our joy; he started whining by the back door. I dragged myself over, and went outside.

It was pretty chilly by now, and the sky was getting

dark. Freedo, however, was enjoying his time. He trotted around the yard, sniffing here and there, barked at a neighbor, and chased the shadow of a bird above.

"Hurry up, boy," I commanded, "I want to go inside."

Freedo looked at me with satisfaction in his face. I could tell he did this to *punish* me for taking Mr. Cuddles away from him. I couldn't believe it.

"What a horrid little dog!"

I dragged him back to the house and slammed the door.

"How could you do this to me, Freedo?!"

He wasn't listening. He just trotted into the living room, towards the piano.

"Don't you dare!"

Seeing that I was watching him, he left the room and splashed some water out of his dog dish.

"Fifty dollars," I reminded myself as I bent my back and dried the floor, *"Just the dog and kids…"*

"Where are the kids?" I froze, *"They were by the table when I left."*

I filled a bowl with water and placed it on the stove to boil. Then I followed the faint sound of fighting upstairs. I opened Laurel's bedroom door to find a disaster.

"What's going on in here?"

It looked like a tornado had hit her room. Laurel was on her bed, surrounded by clothes and dolls, and James was sitting on the floor with tears in his eyes.

"When I came into my room, it looked like this. James messed it up when he was running around with Freedo. I called him here but he won't clean it up!" Laurel complained.

"That's because when Lauwel bwought me herwe, she CUT me.

"WHAT!"

How could all this fighting happen in the short time I was outside with Freedo…. And why would Laurel *cut* her brother?

James rolled up his sleeve and showed me a red scratch.

"Oh, gweat. Now it's bweeding too!" he sobbed

"It's only a scratch James. Let's go downstairs to clean it up."

I brought James downstairs and sat him on the counter top just in time to realize I left a boiling pot of water on the stove.

A Visit Next Door

"Laurel, please come down. I need you to bring me your mom's pasta noodles."

I turned to James, who now managed to crawl to the other end.

"Tha fishies werwe hungwy." He proudly said with an empty can of fish food in his hand.

I peered at the foggy glass of the fish bowl. There were no fish in sight - only a descending grey cloud of mess.

"Your mom didn't say anything about feeding them." I sighed.

"Here are the noodles," Laurel said, heaving the load on the counter.

~

The noodles were cooking (about to be done in a few minutes), and James' scratch was cleaned. I gave the kids a movie to watch and flopped on the sofa to continue reading my book. Again, everything was peaceful.

Freedo jumped on my lap, covering the pages of my book.

"Sorry, boy."

I pushed him off.

Freedo jumped on me again.

"No!" I said crossly

He tried a few more times, but I blocked him with a pillow. Frustrated, he darted and started to run around the room. Tongue hanging out, his little face was twisted in a fury. He was mad. I didn't give in.

Then I looked up from my book, and realized the kids were gone.

"Where are they NOW?!"

I was going nuts. Now Freedo was chewing the piano bench leg. I turned around to see James adding something into the boiling pot of noodles, and Laurel was nowhere in sight.

I was just about to scream when the phone rang.

"Oh my, what if that's Dave?"

In a flash, I turned off the television, peeled the dog from the bench, swooped James off his stool, and grabbed the phone.

"Hello, this is Kat," I breathed out.

"Oh, hello dear," replied Mrs. Peterson, "I was just calling to let you know that I'll be home in ten minutes."

"TEN MINUTES?!"

I put myself together, "Alright, Mrs. Peterson. See

you then!"

I looked around. The stove was a disaster. James' sleeves were dripping wet; Freedo was marching around with someone's underwear. Just then, Laurel joined the scene with a generous amount of lipstick on her face. I wanted to vanish.

"KIDS, we need to work together. Your mom is coming NOW."

They both gave a happy shriek. Freedo dropped the underwear, and we all got to work.

~

When Mrs. Peterson floated through the door, the house was spotless again—except for the cloudy fish bowl. The kids and the dog grouped around their mom as she handed me the reward. I felt elated. What a sense of accomplishment! Just then, I heard her voice saying:

"How about next week…could you watch Freedo for us for three days?"

The End